THE MAN OF THE HOUSE

THE MAN
OF THE HOUSE

by

JOAN FASSLER

Illustrated by Peter Landa

BEHAVIORAL PUBLICATIONS INC., NEW YORK

CHILDREN'S SERIES ON PSYCHOLOGICALLY RELEVANT THEMES

by Joan Fassler

Titles

ALL ALONE WITH DADDY

THE MAN OF THE HOUSE

ONE LITTLE GIRL

Review Committee:

Leonard S. Blackman, Ph.D.
Teachers College, Columbia University

Gerald Caplan, M.D.
Harvard Medical School

Eli M. Bower, Ed.D.
National Institute of
Mental Health

Series Editor:
Sheldon R. Roen, Ph.D.
Teachers College, Columbia University

Production by Bob Vari

Manufactured in the United States of America

Library of Congress Catalog Card Number 73-80122

For my son,
David

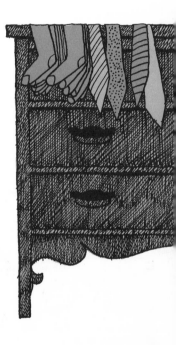

One day David's daddy took one toothbrush, two pairs of pajamas, three sets of underwear, four neckties, five white shirts, six pairs of socks and a very special painting that David had made for him. He put all these things in a grey suitcase.

Then the whole family drove out to the airport, and David's daddy got on a great big airplane. David and his mother waved goodbye to him. And David watched the plane fly far, far away into the sky until he couldn't see it any more at all.

"When will Daddy come home?" asked David that night.

"In a few days," said his mother.

"How long is that?" asked David.

"Maybe four or five days," said his mother.

"But how many sleeps?" asked David.

"I think about four sleeps," said David's mother.

"Oh," said David. "Four more sleeps and Daddy will be home." David pulled up his blankets and hugged his furry brown teddy bear. His mother kissed him goodnight and turned out the light. The house was very quiet.

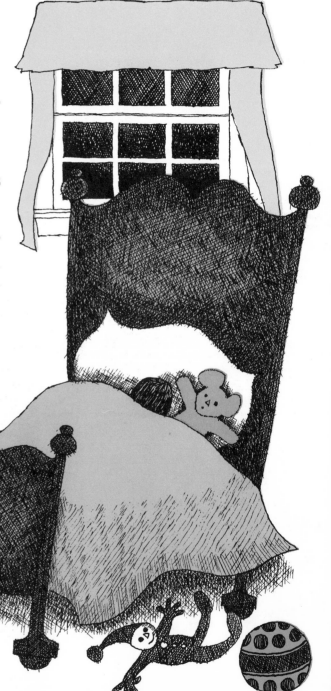

David's mother went downstairs to read. After a while, she glanced up. And there was David — right in the middle of the living room!

"Mommy," said David, "I will be the man of the house while Daddy is away. I will take care of things around here."

"Why, thank you, David. That will be fine," said David's mother.

"Just remember to let me know if you need anything, Mommy. For instance, if a dragon crashes into your room at night and breathes fire right into your face, don't be scared. Just call me."

"I will slash his head off with my magic sword."

"Oh yes," said David's mother. "You will be the first one I will call if any dragons come in to bother me."

"Good," said David. And he went back to bed.

The next night David said to his mother, "Three more sleeps and Daddy will be home. Well, I am still the man of the house around here. Just remember to let me know if you need anything, Mommy. For instance, if a pack of little white wolves crawls into your room and starts to bite your toes with their sharp front teeth, don't be afraid. Just call me."

"I will stamp down on them with my magic boots until they all disappear."

"Oh, yes," said David's mother. "I will certainly call you if I see any little white wolves."

"Good," said David. And he went back to bed.

The next night David said to his mother, "Two more sleeps and Daddy will be home. Well, I am still the man of the house around here. Just remember to let me know if you need anything, Mommy. For instance, if a crocodile slithers into your room and tries to drag you away, don't be scared. Just call me."

"I will spray him with my magic ray
gun."

"Yes, dear," said David's mother. "If I see any crocodiles, I will call you right away."

"Good," said David. And he went to sleep.

The next night David said to his mother, "Only one more sleep and Daddy will be home. Well, I am still the man of the house around here. Just remember to let me know if you need anything, Mommy. For instance, if a hairy hissing monster knocks on the door so hard that the whole house begins to shake, don't be afraid. Just call me."

"I will hurry down with my magic
flame-thrower and burn him up to bits."

"Oh, yes," said David's mother. "You will be the first one I will call if a monster knocks on our door."

"Good," said David. And he curled up and went to sleep.

The next evening David's daddy came home. First he hugged and kissed David's mother. Then he hugged and kissed David. Soon David's daddy opened up his grey suitcase. He took out a great big shiny new paint set for David and a very tiny bottle of perfume for David's mother. He put his toothbrush in the toothbrush holder. He put two pairs of pajamas and three sets of underwear in the hamper. He hung his four neckties back on his tie rack. He put five white shirts in a bundle to go out to the laundry. And he gave David's mother six pairs of socks for her to wash.

At bedtime that night, David's daddy kissed David goodnight. And he wrapped him up gently in his big soft blanket. Then he said to David, "I hear that you took very good care of things around here while I was away. Did you like being the man of the house?"

David thought for a little while. Then he said, "It felt very good to be in charge of things around here, Daddy. But now I am not the man of the house any more. I am just a little boy — your little boy. And that feels good too."

David's daddy smiled at David. Then he turned out the light and walked quietly out of the room.

He went downstairs and sat close to David's mother. The house was very quiet. But all of a sudden there was David — right in the middle of the living room.

"Daddy," said David.

"Yes, David," said David's daddy.

"I guess you will take care of things around here now, won't you? For instance, if any dragons, wolves, crocodiles, or monsters happen to come around to bother us, you will get rid of them pretty quickly, won't you?"

"Yes, David. I will look after things," said David's daddy.

"Good," said David, as he turned around slowly and went back up the stairs.

But somehow, deep down inside himself, David felt just a tiny little bit of sadness. Then David climbed back into his bed and clutched his furry brown teddy bear tightly. And, after a while, David fell fast asleep.

W. Thomson